# The Tale of Mitch or Snitch

## Why you should never put your hands in your pockets

# LAURA BEAUMONT

# The Tale of Mitch or Snitch

## Why you should never put your hands in your pockets

I'M TELLING ON YOO-OU!

Andersen Press · London

*For Minnie Moo and Sarah Broon*
*Forever Friends*

First published in 1994 by
Andersen Press Limited,
20 Vauxhall Bridge Road, London SW1

Phototypeset by Intype, London
Printed and bound in Great Britain by
Mackays of Chatham PLC, Chatham, Kent

British Library Cataloguing in Publication Data is available
ISBN 0 86264 489 5

# Annie Visits Her Grannie

Every fortnight, on a Saturday at 3.30 p.m.
Annie would go to her grannie's house for
tea. But this Saturday things were going to
be a bit different. This Saturday, Grannie was
going to take Annie to the 'Ideal Root Vegetable Exhibition'. For root vegetable fans,
like Grannie, this was the most exciting event
of the year. People from all over the world
came to see the exhibits and compete in
things like: 'The Biggest Carrot Contest',
'The Funniest Shaped Turnip Tournament'
and the 'Best Behaved Beetroot Bonanza'.

Grannie only ever entered one event, and
that was: 'The Swede That Looks Most Like
Its Owner' competition and every year she
won it.

She thought her swedes looked like her because when she planted them, she put a recent photograph of herself in beside each one. But the truth of it was, that her face looked very much like a swede to begin with, although nobody had ever had the heart to tell her this.

Annie was really looking forward to her trip and arrived promptly at her grannie's house at 3.30.

Grannie had already selected this year's swede and had it tucked under her arm ready for the journey.

When they arrived at the exhibition, Annie gasped at the sight of the huge marquee.

There were bands playing songs about

vegetables, people selling vegetable jewellery and ladies encouraging people to try a spray of pungent vegetable perfume. Grannie immediately bought a large bottle of Eau de Turnip and a pair of dangly parsnip earrings.

"The lovely thing about vegetable jewellery..." she explained to Annie as she clipped them on, "is that when it goes out of fashion you can just pop it in a stew! You can't do that with diamonds, can you!"

After a bit of a look around, Grannie suggested that they "sit down for a spot of tea".

"Now, where is the café this year?" she muttered, her tiny eyes darting about, "...ah yes, there it is."

Annie followed her gaze across the tent and there, bright green and shiny and festooned with bunches of gleaming fresh leeks, was the Leek-U-Like Café.

"That looks nice, Grannie," said Annie.

"It does, doesn't it," said Grannie, "... but we're not going there..."

"We're not?"

"No, we're going to the one round the corner, the Leek-U-Don't-Like."

And sure enough, round the corner stood an altogether different sort of café.

"But, Grannie..." whispered Annie.

"Don't you think it looks a bit ... er um ... grubby?"

"Grubby?" snapped Grannie. "Grubby! Of course it looks grubby ... There's nothing worse for you than washed vegetables ... remember, a mouthful of muck and you'll always have good luck."

Annie sighed. Her grannie seemed to be getting madder by the minute. Annie put her hands in her pockets and headed towards the grimy brown canopy.

Suddenly from behind her came a shriek, followed by a terrific crash. Annie turned round just in time to see Grannie rooted to

9

the spot, her
swede spinning
on the ground,
her new parsnip
earrings sticking
up like rabbit's
ears and her
mouth as wide
as a railway
tunnel.

"Grannie, whatever's the matter . . . ?" said
Annie.

A small crowd had gathered.

"P-p-pockets . . ." spluttered Grannie.

"Pockets?" said Annie.

"Your hands – they're in your pockets . . ."

"I know . . ."

"WELL, TAKE THEM OUT!"

Annie did as she was told.

"Don't you know, you must NEVER
NEVER NEVER put your hands in your
pockets!"

The small crowd shook their heads and
tutted.

A portly gentleman holding a turnip

shaped like the Houses of Parliament picked up Grannie's swede and handed it back to her.

"But why not, Grannie?" asked Annie. "Why shouldn't I put my hands in my pockets?"

"Why not?" snapped Grannie, grabbing Annie by the arm and propelling her towards the Leek-U-Don't-Like Café.

"Why not?" she repeated, sitting Annie down on one of the little stools.

"Why not?" she said again, making herself as comfortable as was possible on a seat four times smaller than her bottom.

"What'll it be, Grannie?" grinned the man behind the counter, revealing a row of teeth that looked as if they'd just been used for digging up a flowerbed.

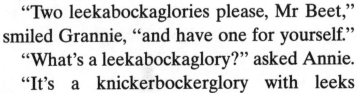

"Two leekabockaglories please, Mr Beet," smiled Grannie, "and have one for yourself."

"What's a leekabockaglory?" asked Annie.

"It's a knickerbockerglory with leeks

instead of knickers . . . now where was I?"

"You were on your third 'why not',
Grannie . . ." prompted Annie.

"Oh yes . . . so I was . . . in that case it must
be time for me to tell you why not."

At that moment
Mr Beet placed a
tall glass in front
of each of them.
They appeared
to contain a
selection of
muddy leeks
and ice cream
scoops.

"Thank you, Mr Beet . . ." smiled Grannie.

Annie looked disbelievingly at her brim-
ming glass. It reminded her of something
she'd once seen stepping out of a spaceship
in a science fiction film.

"The reason why you must never put your
hands in your pockets . . ." began Grannie
sinisterly, ". . . is because of Mitch Snitch."

"Mitch Snitch?" said Annie.

"Mitch Snitch," said Grannie, shovelling an

enormous spoonful of leekabockaglory into her mouth.

And Annie knew, from the way her grannie was staring wistfully into the distance that, as soon as she'd finished chewing, a story would be told . . .

# The Tale of Mitch Snitch

"Mitch Snitch was the most terrible tell-tale," began Grannie.

"Now, in case you don't know, a tell-tale is one of those children who, when you're doing something a bit naughty, will suddenly appear as if from nowhere and say:

'Ooooh . . . I'm telling on you!'

They then rush across to the nearest grown-up, as fast as their horrid little legs will carry them, and tell the tale.

Now, most people know a tell-tale. There's usually one in every school. But, the thing that made Mitch Snitch the sort of tell-tale that people write stories about . . . was her nose. Not only was it as long and poky as a sharpened pencil,

it also had the amazing ability to sniff out naughtiness like a dog sniffs out a bone.

First it would itch, then it would twitch . . .

14

then it would slowly start to bend in the direction that the naughtiness was coming from. Her mouth would then purse up like a prune, her eyes would narrow and suddenly she'd be off! Following her twitching nostrils across the playground towards the naughtiness. Children would throw themselves out of the way, desperate not to be caught in the path of that horrible hooter.

Eventually, when the guilty children were in her sights, her nose would zoom towards them like a rocket heading towards its target.

Usually they'd be too busy doing their naughty thing even to notice her approaching. Then suddenly, something would make

them look up and there she'd be, looming above them like a great skinny scarecrow, a gleam in her eye, and a smile as wide as a very big boomerang.

'Oooooh . . .' she'd squawk, her voice going up and down like a yo-yo.

And before they could even begin to say, 'Oh please don't tell on us, Mitch . . .' she'd be off . . . to find the nearest grown-up. And tell the tale.

Well, as you can imagine, this all made Mitch extremely unpopular. The other children at school called her names (in secret of course), drew horrible pictures of her and wrote poems about her great long nose like:

*There once was a tell-tale called Mitch,*
*Who looked like a prizewinning witch,*
*Her nose was so long,*
*It could pick up a pong,*
*From Papua New Guinea.*

(The children at Mitch's school weren't actually very good at poetry, but they were brilliant at geography and knew that Papua New Guinea was about as far away as you could possibly get.)

Now, I expect you're wondering what Mitch's parents would have said about this nasty little habit of hers. Well, you'll be surprised to hear that they would have said something like this:

In other words they would have been very happy indeed.

You see, Mr and Mrs Snitch were rather snooty, sniffy people, who considered a nice straight parting to be a far better indication of a person's character than a smiley face or a kind pair of eyes. And even then, the parting had to be so straight you could check it with a set-square, which Mr Snitch quite often did.

Mr Snitch felt so strongly about this, that he'd actually started up his very own political party. He called this party the Parting Party and their motto was:

PART IF YOU WANT TO BE SMART
JOIN THE PARTING PARTY

So it will come as no surprise, I'm sure, when I tell you that Mr and Mrs Snitch sent their daughter, Mitch, to Grizzlington Grange."

"What's Grizzlington Grange?" asked Annie.

"You mean to say you don't know?" said Grannie, taking a quick nibble of a nearby leek.

Annie shook her head.

"Well..." began Grannie, in a rather spooky voice, "Grizzlington Grange was just about the strictest school that has ever been. In fact it was so strict, even Fluffy, the school cat, had to wear a uniform...

The building itself was tall and grey with huge iron gates. Bats circled the rooftops and gargoyles peered down from every nook and cranny.

Hideous though these gargoyles were, they looked like everyone's favourite dolly compared to Miss Growler."

"Miss Growler?" said Annie.

20

"The school's headmistress," said Grannie, "and the nearest thing most people had ever seen to a rhinoceros in a dress. (Unless, of course, they'd actually seen a rhinoceros in a dress.)

Now, Grizzlington Grange had more rules and regulations than I've had hot parsnip suppers. And, believe me, that's one heck of a lot. There was the usual 'no talking in class', 'no fidgeting', 'no writing rude words on the school desks' ... but the ones that made the difference were the ones that involved 'having fun'. It was Miss Growler's considered opinion that 'fun' distracted children from their work. So laughing, smiling, pulling silly faces and any kind of playing whatsoever were strictly forbidden.

But perhaps the rule that Miss Growler was most strict about was: NEVER PUT YOUR HANDS IN YOUR POCKETS."

Annie blinked nervously.

" 'Pockets can be the hiding place for toys and games and sweets and other things that might distract a child from learning!' she'd bellow.

In fact, she had a cupboard full of things she'd confiscated from children's pockets.

These ranged from the smallest bouncy ball to an entire toy train set.

Now all this may sound perfectly dreadful, but there was no doubt that it worked. The children learned lots and lots of things. And Grizzlington Grange continued to be one of the top three schools in the country for well-behaved, well-educated children.

It was also a plum place to be for a tell-tale.

# *Other People's Sandwiches*

Now, although Mitch Snitch had been telling tales for quite a long time, she had only just discovered one of the major perks of the job. And that was that, sometimes, if you go up to a child and tell them that you are going to tell on them, they might just say something like:

OH PLEASE MITCH, DON'T TELL ON US, WE'LL GIVE YOU ALL OUR SANDWICHES.

And there was nothing Mitch liked better than other people's sandwiches. So 'sometimes' soon became 'more and more often', which then became 'pretty much all the time'.

This had an almost immediate effect on Mitch's waistline.

Now, Mitch's most favourite tell-taling time was break time. As I said before, 'playing' wasn't actually allowed at Grizzlington Grange. The only things the children could do in the playground were either stand as still as statues eating their sandwiches OR march round and round in a perfect circle reciting their times tables. Which was just as well, as the school playground was not a very pleasant place to be. Miss Growler had made very sure of that.

It was small, covered in huge dangerous

potholes and large clumps of stinging nettles. And it was surrounded by beehives.

In these beehives lived Miss Growler's bees. Now, a very interesting thing had happened to these bees. You see, years and years of seeing all these children reciting times tables every day, had given them a taste for learning. They wanted to be educated – to be allowed to swot, rather than be swatted. Unfortunately Miss Growler never let them fly anywhere near the classrooms. They were considered far too much of a distraction. So they had put their little buzzy heads together and made a plan. This plan was called 'Plan Bee'. And it was so brilliant that in years to come bee film-makers would make films about it."

"Are there really such things as films made by bees?" gasped Annie disbelievingly.

"Of course. Ask your mum and dad if they've ever heard of bee movies and I guarantee they'll say yes."

"Okay," said Annie, "I will."

"Anyway," continued Grannie. "Back to 'Plan Bee'. Firstly, the bees were going to make a life-sized model of Fluffy the school cat out of beeswax.

Secondly, they would climb inside.

Thirdly, they would propel the beeswax Fluffy through the school grounds, in through the door and then into one of the classrooms.

Fourthly, they would stand at the back of the class and learn things.

You see, the bees knew that nobody ever

took any notice of Fluffy the school cat. Miss Growler had chosen him especially. In fact, Fluffy was the least fluffy thing most people had ever seen. One would have been more tempted to stroke a piece of cheese.

So anyway, that was the plan and all the bees in the hive were very excited about it.

Well, as the days and weeks went by, Mitch was getting plumper and plumper and greedier and greedier. She was now not just content with waiting for her nose to sniff out the odd bit of naughtiness. She'd taken to playing the most terrible tricks.

She'd drop bulgy toys into the children's pockets when they weren't looking, and whisper really funny jokes into their ears so they'd start laughing. Sometimes she'd even hum jolly country music so they'd start skipping about.

And then, when they did all these naughty things, she'd say: 'Ooooh! I'm telling on you!'

And, more often than not, sandwiches would change hands.

Now, this particular day, Miss Growler was sitting in her office planting more tufts of hair into her eyebrows so she'd look even more fierce, when suddenly a letter arrived.

Letters didn't arrive very often at Grizzlington Grange. This was mainly because postmen find it very hard to approach a letter box without whistling a jolly song, and Miss Growler hated jolly songs. The only songs she liked were slow droney ones, preferably about terrible things that happened to poor hapless children. In fact the school hymn began

'Little Johnny Pincer fell into a mincer ...'

This was the un-jolliest song that had ever been written. And it was so slow, the pianist quite often fell asleep between notes.

Miss Growler loved it. She sang along as tunelessly as she could, in her booming foghorn of a voice.

The reason Miss Growler hated jolly songs was because they made her feel sick. Simple as that. And the sight of Miss Growler feeling sick was not one any self-respecting postman would want to see twice.

First her eyes would bulge out like billiard balls.

Then her tongue would suddenly roll out of her mouth like one of those squeaky blowers you get at parties.

And for the grand finale, her tongue would roll in and out while she made a noise like a cat trying to cough up a fur ball.

So, to avoid this hideous spectacle, post-men were advised to put huge corks in their mouths when deliver-ing to Grizzlington Grange to stop them-selves from whistling, at  least until they were well clear of the driveway.

Miss Growler sat back on her chair and opened the letter. It said:

**Dear Miss Growler,**

**I have great pleasure in informing you that Grizzlington Grange has been nominated to receive the Golden Grimace award for discipline.**

**Mr Grub, our chief school inspector, will be calling next Wednesday to assess your suit-ability to receive such a coveted trophy.**

**Yours faithfully,**

D. Dour

Miss Growler was so excited she nearly stopped scowling. You see, the Golden Grimace was the highest award a school like Grizzlington Grange could get. It would mean that almost overnight they would become the most famous strict school in the country and parents from all over the world would be clamouring to send their children there. Which, of course, would mean lots more money for Miss Growler.

'I can put more potholes in the playground,' she gasped, 'get even more uncomfortable chairs for the pupils to sit on and [and this was her biggest dream] get a whole orchestra to play the morning rendition of *Little Johnny Pincer Fell into a Mincer*!'

The mere thought of it brought a tear to her crinkled old eye.

'Nothing must go wrong in front of that inspector! NOTHING!' she boomed. 'If he gets one niff of naughtiness we're finished. What I need is an extra pair of eyes – or should I say – NOSE!'

And with that she immediately summoned Mitch Snitch to her office.

Mitch marched in and stood to attention just as she was supposed to.

'Snitch,' said Miss Growler slimily, 'I have always considered you to be one of my most devious and sneaky informers.'

Oh yes, never think for a second that teachers don't know about tell-tales. In the world of schools, a teacher's tell-tale is considered to be just about as important as their chalk – but don't tell them I told you."

Annie shook her head.

"Miss Growler continued, 'In a few days' time, I am going to need the assistance of that disobedience detecting beak of yours. And if all goes well, Snitch, YOU will be the new Grizzlington Grange head girl!'

'Head girl!' gasped Mitch.

'Yes, head girl!' snapped Miss Growler. 'Now, get out!'

'Yes, Miss Growler, thank you, Miss Growler!'

Mitch marched out of the office and down the stairs.

'Head girl!' she gasped. 'Of Grizzlington Grange . . .'

Mitch was excited. Very excited. Not only would she soon be the proud owner of a shiny new badge, but she would also have the power to be even more bossy, tell even more tales and, most important of all, eat even more sandwiches! But then why just stop at sandwiches?

'Today sandwiches . . .' she whispered to herself as she marched out into the playground.

'Tomorrow – puddings, pies and big squadgy cakes!'

At the mere thought of all that stodge, the button of her skirt gave a little tiny tug.

# The Big Day

Well, the big day came, as big days always do, and every child in Grizzlington Grange was under strict instructions to look their smartest.

Now smartness was getting a bit difficult for Mitch Snitch. All her skirts were now so tight they made her look like a balloon with an elastic band round the middle.

This is something you rather hope your parents will see and either a) buy you a new skirt or b) sew an extra panel in your old one. Mr and Mrs Snitch did neither. They were far too busy putting the finishing touches to Mr Snitch's political party song even to notice.

Now, coincidentally enough, this was also a very big day for the bees. The beeswax Fluffy was finished and already the bees were excitedly queuing up to get inside. Actually, the making of the lifelike model had been quite easy; it was the kidnapping and keeping prisoner of the real Fluffy that was proving to be a bit tricky.

On the stroke of nine o'clock Mr Grub the school inspector arrived.

He was a very small skinny man whose suit was so baggy it could have easily fitted in another person.

'Please try and pretend I'm not here,' he told Miss Growler, his jaw cracking like a bag of conkers. She gave a knowing wink to Mitch Snitch and the day began.

Mr Grub followed the children from class to class, tutting and muttering and scribbling things down on his dusty old clipboard. Occasionally he'd stop to measure the straightness of a back or the smartness of a march. But his expression never changed. It 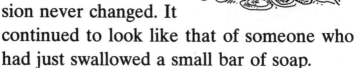 continued to look like that of someone who had just swallowed a small bar of soap.

Mitch was also on the lookout for any disobedience, and had already managed to secretly scoff away four rounds of the very best cheese and pickle.

The last lesson of the day was about to begin when Mr Grub sidled up to Miss Growler.

'It is customary at this time,' he began, 'to give you an indication of my findings.'

'And?' said Miss Growler anxiously.

'If this standard of discipline is upheld, the award is as good as yours.'

Miss Growler gave a small croak.

'One class away from the Golden Grimace,' she thought. 'What could possibly go wrong?'

Just outside the window, something that looked remarkably like Fluffy the school cat was crossing the playground. Except that instead of miaowing . . . it was buzzing.

The last lesson of the day was science, a subject that Miss Growler was particularly

keen on. She found that children always behaved very well around substances that could make a very big bang at any moment. And the Grizzlington Grange science room was certainly full of those.

'For today's experiment I will be requiring the assistance of my soon-to-be head girl – Mitch Snitch.'

Miss Growler figured that with Mitch out front, keeping an eye on everyone, things were bound to go smoothly.

Mitch sprang proudly to her feet, and marched to the front of the class. Her knees jabbing up so high they nearly touched her nose.

'Soon-to-be head girl,' she thought, sneering round at the watching class. 'I bet those wimps are wishing they were me . . .'

In fact the whole class was thinking the exact opposite.

'Excuse me while I select the chemicals,' said Miss Growler. And with a mutter of 'Now do we want a very big bang or a very nasty smell . . .' she turned round and began to rummage about in her chemicals cupboard.

Mitch was feeling proud. And when she felt proud she puffed up like a preening pigeon. First her cheeks, and then her chest, and her preening would have gone on and on, but unfortunately, the button on her skirt chose this moment to give up trying to hold on any longer.

With the biggest ping that had ever been recorded in the history of pings, the button flew across the room hitting poor Mr Grub right between the eyes.

He dropped like a stone.

In a trice, Mitch's smirky expression had changed to one of complete and utter horror. With her button gone, her skirt would almost certainly fall down and that was the last thing she wanted to happen – especially in front of the whole class *and* Miss Growler *and indeed* the school inspector (if he ever got up again).

So, she did the first thing that came into her head (which was probably not the most sensible). She plunged her hands into her pockets to stop her skirt from falling to the floor.

Well, this was a sight every child at Grizzlington Grange had dreamed of. Mitch Snitch breaking the most important school rule of all. They nearly cheered.

'Get up, get up . . .' thought the class, looking round at the prostrate school inspector.

'Don't get up . . . don't get up . . .' thought Mitch as she struggled to free her hands from her pockets. But it was no good. Because of her little fat tummy, her hands were well and truly stuck.

And all the while Miss Growler rummaged noisily through her chemicals, unaware of the drama that was beginning to unfold.

Mitch lurched from one side to another, pulling and tugging like an escapologist trying to get out of a straitjacket.

Suddenly Miss Growler spoke: 'Ah that should do it . . .'

'Oh no,' thought Mitch, 'she's going to get up, she's going to turn round!' And, with that, she gave one last huge pull.

The class watched in amazement as Mitch flew back in a spectacular back somersault, lost her balance and plummeted, nose first, into Miss Growler's upended bottom.

There was an almighty scream followed by

a crash as the gargantuan headmistress top-
pled into the chemicals cupboard.

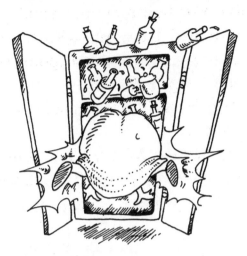

The class gasped.

Mitch steadied herself and peered nervously into the cupboard.

There was a clattering and a tinkling and
suddenly Miss Growler emerged, like a huge
swamp monster. She was covered from head
to toe in potions and powders and she was
rubbing her rear end.

It wouldn't have taken an expert in anger
to see that she was angry.

'SNITCH!' she bellowed.

But Mitch was looking past her, into the

cupboard – at the sparks and the smoke.

You see, mixing up just two of these chemicals made a big bang. But mixing all of them together – well, it didn't bear thinking about.

'Um . . . Miss Growler . . .' muttered Mitch feebly, jabbing her, now slightly bent, nose in the direction of the sizzling mess at the bottom of the cupboard.

'DON'T YOU JAB THAT THING AT ME!' screamed the enraged headmistress.

'No, Miss Growler,' urged Mitch. 'Look behind you!'

So Miss Growler looked. And then looked back.

'I think we'd better all get out,' she gasped, 'NOW!'

With that the entire class clattered to their feet and bundled squealing towards the door.

The cupboard began to fizz.

Miss Growler suddenly looked around.

'Hang on, where's Mr Grub, and what's that horrible old suit doing on the floor . . . Oh my goodness . . . that *is* Mr Grub!'

At the sound of his name the poor man sat up. 'What happened?' he muttered, small birds tweeting in a circle round his head.

'Nothing, absolutely nothing. You're dreaming, Mr Grub,' said Miss Growler, thinking fast. And with that, she picked him up and threw him across her shoulders.

Meanwhile two floors down, a large white cat in a small school uniform had just crossed the threshold. The bees were feeling very pleased with themselves. They'd got the beeswax Fluffy through the main entrance unseen and were now heading towards the art room ready for their first lesson.

Upstairs, every child in Miss Growler's class was now standing outside on the landing. Miss Growler was the last one out of the, now very smoky, science room. She fell through the door with Mr Grub dangling round her neck like a fur stole.

Her eyes flicked from child to child. 'Snitch . . .' she snarled. 'Where's SNITCH?'

The class happily parted to reveal the snivelling Snitch.

Luckily for Mitch, before Miss Growler could snarl another word the science cupboard exploded.

The huge smelly blast blew everyone off their feet and down the stairs. It was like a waterfall of children, rolling, sliding and cartwheeling down the huge winding Grizzlington Grange staircase. Mitch, her hands still hopelessly wedged in her pockets, zoomed down the middle like a turbo-charged penguin. She was followed closely by Miss Growler, who was now doing spectacular roly polys, with Mr Grub hanging on like a baby baboon. 'This is really one of the most unpleasant dreams I think I've ever had,' he muttered.

Everyone landed in a huge squirming heap at the bottom of the stairs. Everyone, except

Mitch, who
had got up such
a speed, she just continued
zooming straight across the school entrance
hall.

Suddenly she came to a rather abrupt halt. Her kebab skewer of a nose had buried itself in something soft. Something that smelled rather sweet.

Mitch staggered to her feet (which was really quite difficult with no hands). A very peculiar object seemed to be stuck to the end of her nose. She tried crossing her eyes to see it but all she could make out was some kind of white blob in what appeared to be a school blazer.

'What on earth is it?' she thought to herself.

Which, oddly enough, was exactly what the bees thought when the pink pointy thing burst through the walls of their lovely bees-wax Fluffy."

"Oh no . . ." gasped Annie.

"Oh yes . . ." smiled Grannie.

# From Bad to Worse

" 'What's that she's got on the end of her nose?' said one child.

'Um . . . I think it's Fluffy the school cat,' said another.

'THE SCHOOL CAT?' yelped Mitch, feeling ever so slightly queasy.

'Oh gross . . .' said some other children.

'Just a minute,' came Miss Growler's unmistakable booming tones, as she struggled free from the tangle of arms and legs. 'You can't have the school cat stuck to the end of your nose. It's not allowed!'

'School cat? . . . Nose?' muttered Mr Grub, who, despite the spectacular tumble, still appeared to be draped around Miss Growler's shoulders.

'No, just a minute,' said the first child. '*There's* the school cat.'

And everybody looked, and everybody saw – Fluffy the real school cat silhouetted in the doorway like an avenging hero.

(Bees may be great at making models out of beeswax, but they're useless at tying cats up.)

Everyone stared at the cat in the doorway, then they all looked back at Mitch, and then they all looked back at the doorway again.

'If that's Fluffy the school cat . . .' gibbered Mitch, feeling even more queasy, 'then what have I got on the end of my . . .'

But before she could gibber the word 'nose', Fluffy had given a bloodcurdling wail and leapt up into the air. Mitch watched in horror, as two and a half pounds of angry pussycat sailed towards her.

Fluffy made a perfect landing on top of the beeswax cat. Children scattered in all directions leaving Mitch to stare cross-eyed at the totem pole of cats that now seemed to be balanced on the end of her nose.

Now Fluffy was a fighter (which is one reason he hated his name so much). He wanted revenge for having been catnapped.

But more than that, he wanted his school blazer back.

He grabbed hold of the collar with his teeth and began to pull.

Inside the beeswax Fluffy, the bees were panicking. 'Abandon cat!' they buzzed. 'Abandon cat!'

Mitch did the only thing she could think of, which was to squeak rather feebly:

'Um, hello, could someone get these um cats off my nose?'

Unfortunately, years of having their sandwiches pinched and tales told on them did not make the children very sympathetic to

Mitch's plight. They all just stood and stared, fascinated to see what on earth was going to happen next.

Suddenly Fluffy gave a triumphant 'miaow' and fell to the floor, the school blazer dangling from his mouth.

If he could have said, 'Ah hah! That'll teach you to mess with Fluffy!' he probably would have. Unfortunately, he couldn't. So he didn't.

Mitch was relieved that one cat was gone. But there was still the other, which had quite alarmingly started to buzz.

Suddenly, there was a squelch and a small flap opened in the beeswax Fluffy's tummy.

Out flew the bees.

'Bees!' screeched the children.

'BEES!' bellowed Miss Growler.

'Bees!' squeaked Mitch Snitch.

'Bees?' gasped Mr Grub, who had decided he'd had enough of this nightmare, and was now in the process of pinching himself to try and wake up.

The air was suddenly full of confused buzzing bees, all of which seemed to be coming from the thing on Mitch's nose.

'I KNOW THOSE BEES!' roared Miss Growler. 'Those are *my* bees! Where's my swatter . . . where's my swatter?'

With that she flipped Mr Grub on to the floor, grabbed his clipboard, and began swiping.

Now, bees don't like it when they're swiped at. And it was rather unfortunate that the instruction 'Abandon cat' also meant 'Arm yourselves with honeybombs'!"

"Honeybombs?" said Annie.

"Don't you know anything about bees?" snapped Grannie. "Honeybombs are like water bombs ... except they're made with honey! Bees use them so they don't have to use their stings because if they use their stings they die! Okay?"

"Okay," said Annie, vowing not to ask Grannie another question. Especially about bees.

" 'Honeybomb everything!' buzzed the bee commander. 'Except the rhinoceros with the clipboard. That one's mine!'

And with that they began to fly about dropping the bombs on anything that moved. And, believe me, things were moving. Children were running, Miss Growler was

swiping, Fluffy was struggling back into his blazer and Mitch was frantically trying to shake the remains of the beeswax Fluffy off the end of her nose.

Perhaps the only exception was Mr Grub. He had stopped pinching himself, and was now beginning to look rather cross.

Now, a very peculiar thing was beginning

to happen. Although the children were scampering about squealing, trying to get away from the bees, they found that they were actually beginning to enjoy themselves. It had been a very long time since they'd played chase, and they'd forgotten what good fun it was, especially when you are being bombarded by sticky honeybombs.

First they began to giggle, then they began to chuckle and before they knew it they were all falling about and laughing loudly.

Mitch was most definitely not laughing. She had decided that if she twirled round in a circle very very fast the beeswax blob might just fly off her nose. With her hands still wedged in her pockets, it was really all she could do. So she began to spin.

Faster and faster she spun. And we all know what happens when you start to spin. You start to move about.

Mitch twirled past the sticky children, past the swatting Miss Growler and past the smirking Fluffy. Then suddenly, there was a huge loud slurping noise, and the beeswax cat was gone.

'Phew!' she thought, and would have loved nothing better than to have stopped spinning and breathed a sigh of relief. Unfortunately, she was now turning so fast, she couldn't stop.

The sight of the school tell-tale twirling past them like a spinning top made the children laugh even more, especially as the air whizzing through her huge flappy nostrils was now beginning to play a tune. They didn't even stop laughing when she spun straight into the huge cupboard on the other side of the hall and smashed through the two pad-locked doors.

Now, this might have been all right if this

had been an ordinary cupboard, full of books or pencils. Unfortunately, it wasn't. Do you remember me mentioning a cupboard where Miss Growler kept all the toys she'd confiscated from children's pockets?"

Annie nodded nervously.

"Well, this was that very cupboard!" beamed Grannie. "As Mitch Snitch fell in, all the toys fell out.

Balls bounced, hula hoops rolled, frisbees flew and toy cars zoomed. And because the children were all so sticky, all the toys stuck to them. So now, the children were not only running around laughing, they were also covered in toys.

They looked at each other and laughed; they looked at Mitch Snitch and laughed; they even looked at Miss Growler and laughed. Even the bees were laughing (although nobody except a bee expert would have known).

But then suddenly, in the midst of all this jollity, there came a very strange sound. A muffled tutting sound.

Now, you may be wondering what had happened to the beeswax Fluffy after it left Mitch's nose. It could have fallen on the floor, or flown out of the window or even splattered against the wall. Unfortunately, it hadn't done any of those things. It had done the most terrible thing possible. It had hit poor Mr Grub full in the face.

As far as the school inspector was concerned, this was the last in a very long line of straws. He now stood in the centre of the room tutting very loudly, the beeswax cat sitting on his head, like a very sticky balaclava helmet.

'Oh no . . .' gasped Miss Growler, stopping her swatting and looking round.

One by one, everyone became as still as

statues. Even the bees just seemed to hover where they were.

'Oh,' spluttered Miss Growler, trying to be pleasant to the enraged inspector. 'You're awake then.'

'AWAKE!' boomed Mr Grub. 'AWAKE! I'll have you know, my good madam, that I have never been ASLEEP! That was just some outrageous untruth that you made up, to make me think that the hideous goings-on at this pathetic excuse for a strict school weren't really happening!'

With that, he snatched back his clipboard. Miss Growler gasped.

'I have seen things today, Miss Growler, things that belong in school inspectors' night-mares. I have seen children rolling down stairs, sliding down banisters, running, screaming, laughing, playing with toys, a child with a cat on the end of her nose but even worse than that – a child with her hands in her pockets. By my accounting, the only school rule these disgraceful children have managed to avoid breaking is rule number 164: pulling a funny face! So what do you have to say, Miss Growler? What do you have to say?'

At that moment the doorbell rang. Miss Growler strode to the door and opened it.

Standing there, surrounded by a group of people with partings so straight, headlice could ride bicycles down them, were Mr and Mrs Snitch.

Suddenly, and with no warning at all, they began to sing a very jolly song;

Now every single child in the school knew what happened when Miss Growler heard a jolly song. Each and every one of them looked across at her. But more unfortunately, so did Mr Grub.

First her eyes began to bulge like billiard balls, then her tongue began to roll out of her mouth like one of those squeaky blowers you get at parties. It was at this point that Mr Grub decided to leave. By the time Miss Growler's tongue was rolling in and out of her mouth and she was making a sound like a cat trying to cough up a fur ball, the school inspector was halfway down the drive.

So, Grizzlington Grange never did receive the Golden Grimace. In fact, word got out about the events that took place on that certain Wednesday and every parent came and took their child away. The school was then closed down and made into a supermarket.

And poor Mitch Snitch never became head girl. Neither did she get any puddings, pies or big squadgy cakes. She too was marched from the school, and the only job she ever managed to get was that of a wobbly parting spotter for her father's political party.

YOU'VE GOT A WOBBLY PARTING, I'M TELLING ON YOO-OU!

73

And all because she put her hands in her pockets."

"Wow . . ." said Annie, sensing that Grannie's story was at an end. "But, Grannie, that's not all true, is it? There aren't really schools like Grizzlington Grange, and cats that wear school uniforms and headmistresses that don't even allow you to laugh . . . are there?"

Grannie smiled a familiar knowing smile.

"Two things . . ." she began. "Do you remember that blazer that Fluffy was so keen to get back?"

Annie nodded.

"Well here it is . . ."

Annie gasped as Grannie pulled a small brown blazer out of her handbag. On the collar were two little teeth marks.

"And I expect you're wondering what became of Miss Growler, aren't you?"

"You haven't got her in there too have you, Grannie?" gasped Annie, nodding down at the old brown handbag.

"No, no, no. Take a little peep into Mr Beet's kitchen."

Annie peered into the dank little room at the back of the café.

Through the piles of muddy vegetables, past the racks of steaming plates, a figure stood hunched over the sink. A figure that, even from the back, looked very much like a rhinoceros in a dress.

Annie gasped. "Miss Growler!"

Grannie smiled. "Ssssh, listen!"

Annie listened. The figure was muttering to herself:

"Come on, you plates! Stop looking so shiny. You'll distract the customers from their food! And you, knives and forks, stand up straight! Come along now, sing with me . . .

Little Johnny Pincer fell into a mincer..."

"Oh dear..." said Annie.

"Oh dear indeed," said Grannie, clambering down from her uncomfortable stool. "Come on now, we'd best be off. The Swede That Looks Most Like Its Owner Competition is about to begin."

"Grannie," said Annie, jumping down beside her.

"Yes, Annie?" said Grannie.

"I'll never put my hands in my pockets again!"

And do you know something . . . she never did.